BOO COW

Patricia Baehr

Margot Apple

Charlesbridge

For Riley—P. B.

For Mary Koncel and Dick Wagner—M. A.

First paperback edition 2012
Text copyright © 2010 by Patricia Baehr
Illustrations copyright © 2010 by Margot Apple

Published by Charlesbridge
85 Main Street
Watertown, MA 02472
(617) 926-0329
www.charlesbridge.com

Library of Congress Cataloging-in-Publication Data
Baehr, Patricia Goehner.
   Boo Cow / Patricia Baehr ; illustrated by Margot Apple.
      p. cm.
   Summary: When Mr. and Mrs. Noodleman start a chicken farm, they are
terrorized by a ghostly cow that seems to be keeping the hens from laying
any eggs, but upon further investigation they discover the real culprit.
   ISBN 978-1-58089-108-0 (reinforced for library use)
   ISBN 978-1-58089-299-5 (softcover)
[1. Cows—Fiction. 2. Chickens—Fiction. 3. Ghosts—Fiction. 4. Farm life—Fiction.
5. Humorous stories.] I. Apple, Margot, ill. II. Title.
PZ7.B1387Bo 2010
[E]—dc22   2008025333

Printed in Singapore
(hc) 10 9 8 7 6 5 4 3 2 1
(sc) 10 9 8 7 6 5 4 3 2 1

Illustrations done in #2 lead pencil and pastel pencil on Stonehenge paper
Display type and text type set in KlunderScript and Meridien
Color separations by Chroma Graphics, Singapore
Printed and bound February 2012 by Imago in Singapore
Production supervision by Brian G. Walker
Designed by Susan Mallory Sherman and Diane Earley

Boo Cow had lived a happy life. Each day after the first milking, when the eggs had been collected and the farmer had thumped open the barn doors and swung wide the gate, Molly, as she was called then, had lovingly guided the rest of the milking herd to pasture. But all that was long, long ago. . . .

Mr. and Mrs. Noodleman dreamed of being farmers.
After years of saving they packed up their apartment in
the city and moved to the country.

"Home sweet home!" Mrs. Noodleman announced.

"Well," Mr. Noodleman hedged, "home, anyway."

Mrs. Noodleman set to work fixing the tractor. In time she plowed the fields and planted seeds.

Mr. Noodleman repaired the house and cleaned out the barn. He gave the henhouse a new roof and a coat of pickle-green paint.

Together they fenced the chicken yard and stocked up on Super A-One Top Choice Chicken Feed.

On the day a truck delivered 552 chickens, Mr. Noodleman kissed his wife on the nose. "By tomorrow," he said, "we'll be up to our eyeballs in eggs!"

But in the morning all they found was one egg on the floor, with a crack running down its side.

The next day was the same.

The day after that there were no eggs at all. The Noodlemans couldn't imagine what they were doing wrong.

Mr. Noodleman walked down the road to ask Farmer Hackett's advice. Farmer Hackett's eyes widened. "It's not you," he said. "It's the ghost! Every night at the stroke of twelve, Boo Cow haunts your farm! The chickens must be too scared to lay eggs!"

Was it true? Could the farm be haunted?

EGGS

HACKETT'S

HACKETT

FARM FRESH EGGS

OPEN DAILY

The Noodlemans had been too exhausted to ever stay up past nine. But that evening they tuned in to a six-episode marathon of *Famous Farmers*.

The bedroom was eerily quiet when Mr. Noodleman turned off the television. In the hall, the grandfather clock began to gong. One, two, three times the clock struck.

Thump went something in the barn. . . .

Four, five, six. Creaaak went the chicken-yard gate. . . .

Seven, eight, nine. A cowbell softly tolled,

Clink-clunk! Clink-clunk!

Ten, eleven, twelve.

Mrs. Noodleman shrieked, "That came from the henhouse!"

"It's no wonder the chickens don't lay eggs!" said Mr.

Noodleman. "We must get rid of that horrible Boo Cow!"

But how?

Mr. Noodleman hung garlic from the chicken-yard fence.

Mrs. Noodleman went into town to visit a psychic.

"Boo Cow, Boo Cow, tell us why you haunt the Noodleman farm!" begged the lady with one earring.

Boo Cow didn't answer. But each night the frightened Noodlemans heard her weird moos. And each morning there were no eggs.

"We stink!" Mr. Noodleman said with a stamp of his foot.
"Five hundred and fifty-two chickens and we can't even eat eggs
for breakfast!"

Mrs. Noodleman tried to make her husband feel better. "The
plants are growing, Poppy, and tomorrow, by gum, you shall
have your eggs!" *Even,* she promised herself, *if I have to stand in
line at Hackett's to buy them.*

After dinner Mrs. Noodleman brought four chickens into the farmhouse and settled them in the bedroom atop her favorite fluffy pink nightgown. "Maybe here, away from Boo Cow, they'll lay their eggs."

At midnight the Noodlemans heard the thump in the barn, the creak of the gate, and the terrible clanging of Boo Cow's bell.

Ten, eleven, twelve gongs of the clock . . .

Did Boo Cow sound closer? Mrs. Noodleman looked with alarm at Mr. Noodleman. "Oh, dear!" he said, his breath clouding the suddenly cold room.

To Mr. and Mrs. Noodleman's horror, two wide nostrils
appeared on the bedroom wall! The nostrils loomed closer
as a bell came into view along with two outstretched and
bony hooves. Slowly, silently, the rest of Boo Cow slid
through the wall and into the Noodlemans' bedroom. As she
floated across the room, sighing pitifully, both Noodlemans
dove under the bedcovers.

Mrs. Noodleman could hear the chickens clucking. How could she hide beneath the covers and leave those defenseless chickens to the ghost?

"Stop it, Boo Cow!" she squeaked. "Your ugly mug has frightened its last chicken! Scram! Hit the road! And don't come back!"

Boo Cow made a different sort of noise—was it a sob? She tucked the nightgown snugly around the chickens, kissed the tops of their feathery heads, and faded into the night.

It was some time before the Noodlemans
dared lift the covers. When Mrs. Noodleman was
sure the ghost was gone, she crowed, "I've done it!
No more Boo Cow!"

"No breakfast, either," Mr. Noodleman fretted.
"I bet those terrorized chickens won't lay eggs
for a week."

He was wrong.

"Eggs Benedict," Mrs. Noodleman announced, presenting Mr. Noodleman with breakfast.

Mr. Noodleman happily tucked a napkin under his chin. "With Boo Cow gone, we'll be running a regular egg factory. Why, we might even be as successful as Farmer Hackett someday!"

But he was wrong again. Even with Boo Cow banished there were no eggs in the henhouse the next morning or any other morning that week. Why, then, did the bedroom chickens continue to lay eggs?

Hoping to please the henhouse chickens, Mrs. Noodleman bought every fluffy pink nightgown she could find. Mr. Noodleman indulged them with their very own television. Nothing helped!

"Could it be *us* that the bedroom chickens like?" Mrs. Noodleman wondered.

In the end there was nothing to do but move the bed into the henhouse.

The Noodlemans slept peacefully through midnight, undisturbed by any bovine ghost. But just before dawn, something else roused them.

BOK BOK! BAAAAHK!!!

"Let me drive the tractor," Mr. Noodleman murmured, not yet fully awake.

"Poppy!" hissed Mrs. Noodleman. "Someone's here!"

A sneaky someone who didn't make thumps or creaks or clunks. Someone who didn't moo!

An egg smashed to the henhouse floor. "Drat," said a very unghostlike voice.

Mrs. Noodleman had the lights on in a flash. "Why, it's Farmer Hackett, the dirty old thief! He was stealing the eggs each morning after Boo Cow was gone. Poppy, don't let him get away!"

Mrs. Noodleman called the police while Mr. Noodleman lunged for the intruder. Too late! Farmer Hackett had reached the henhouse door.

"Oh, thank you, Boo Cow!" Mrs. Noodleman cried. "I do believe you were looking out for the chickens all along—please forgive us!"

Boo Cow didn't answer. She grew fainter, then fainter still, and had nearly vanished by the time the police arrived.

"How could we have been so mean to Boo Cow?" Mrs. Noodleman asked her husband sadly. "Do you think she'll ever come back?"

The day dragged on as the Noodlemans waited to see if Boo Cow would return. At last it was midnight. The clock gonged one, two, three—

"Was that a thump?" asked Mr. Noodleman hopefully.

Four, five, six. The Noodlemans strained their ears, hoping to hear a creak.

Seven, eight, nine. No clink-clunk.

Ten, eleven, twelve. Silence.

Mr. Noodleman shook his head sadly. "Perhaps she's never coming back."

But then they heard it—a soft but unmistakable

"Oh, Boo Cow!" cried Mrs. Noodleman. "Welcome home!"